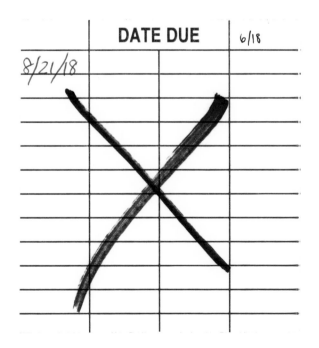

Whiffy Wilson

the wolf who wouldn't go to school

For the children of Meridian Primary School, Peacehaven.
Well done with your fantastic reading. Keep it up!–C.H

To Molly and Jack–L.L

First edition for the United States and Canada published in 2015
by Barron's Educational Series, Inc.

First published in 2014 by Orchard Books

Text © Caryl Hart 2014
Illustrations © Leonie Lord 2014

All inquiries should be addressed to:
Barron's Educational Series, Inc.
250 Wireless Boulevard
Hauppauge, NY 11788
www.barronseduc.com

Library of Congress Control Number: 2014942873
ISBN: 978-1-4380-0620-8

Date of Manufacture: March 2017
Manufactured by: RRD Asia Printing Solution Limited, China

Printed in China
9 8 7 6 5 4 3 2

Whiffy Wilson

The Wolf who wouldn't go to school

Caryl Hart  BARRON'S Leonie Lord

There was a wolf named Wilson
Who couldn't count to ten.
He wouldn't learn to write his name.
He never used a pen.

He didn't know his ABCs.

He couldn't paint or cook.

He wouldn't learn his two-plus-twos.

He never read a book.

"Time for

School!"

his father cried,

"You pesky little pup!"

"But school is **BORING!**" Wilson whined,
And he turned the TV up.

One morning, Wilson went next door
To ask his friend to play.
But Dotty smiled, "I can't because
I'm off to school today."

"Well, *I'm* not going," Wilson grumped.
"Who wants to read and write?
I'd rather play and watch TV
And stay up late at night."

"Oh, you're so silly," Dotty smiled.
"Come to school with me!
There's nothing to be scared of–
School's lots of fun, you'll see!"

"WHO SAYS I'M SCARED?"
growled Wilson.
"A wolf is brave and strong.
It's just … the teacher might be mad
If I get the answers wrong."

But Dotty wasn't worried,
She just grabbed him by the paw.
She marched him up the path to school
And pushed him through the door.

She hung his coat up on a hook,
She made him use the bathroom,
Then took him to the classroom
And showed him what to do.

"First you paint a picture
And stick it on the wall."

"Then you get some cookie dough
And roll it in a ball.
You squeeze it and you squash it
And you pat it nice and flat,

Then get some cookie cutters
And make a shape—like that!"

"Next you get the ladybugs
And count up all the spots.
Then we'll draw a picture
By joining up these dots."

At lunchtime they had pizza,
Then ran to play outside.
"Let's play soccer!" called a boy.
"My favorite!" Wilson cried.

He ran and passed and dribbled,
Then he scored a goal—hooray!
His team cheered, "Whiffy Wilson,
You're the Hero of the Day!"

"I thought no one would like me,"
Said Wilson with a grin.
"But look at all my lovely friends.
It's great fun joining in."

During arts and crafts that afternoon
They made a flying car.
"What lovely work," the teacher smiled.
"You've earned a golden star."

Dotty | Wilson

"This isn't work!" gasped Wilson.
"All we've done so far is play!"
"Oh, you're so funny," Dotty laughed.
"We've been working hard all day!"

But the day was nearly over
So they sat down on the rug.
The teacher read a story
And Wilson gave his friend a hug.

"This school is perfect," Wilson grinned,
"It isn't dull at all.
I can play with all the other kids.
I can run and kick a ball!"

"The classroom toys are really cool.
The teacher is so kind.
If I had to come here every day,
I really wouldn't mind!"

Next morning, Whiffy Wilson
Was up and dressed at eight.
He called for Dotty right away,
"It's school—we can't be late!"

"Oh, Whiffy Wilson," Dotty smiled.
"You really are the best!
There's no school on a *Saturday*—
It's time to take a rest!"

"But home is BORING!" Wilson whined.
"I want to go and play.
What can I do? Just stay inside
And watch TV all day?"

"Never mind," smiled Dotty.
"You can come and play with me."

So they ran around the backyard,
As happy as can be.

the end.